THE ADVENTURES OF
WRONG MAN
AND
POWER GIRL!

WORDS BY
C. ALEXANDER LONDON

ILLUSTRATED BY
FRANK MORRISON

PHILOMEL BOOKS

PHILOMEL BOOKS
an imprint of Penguin Random House LLC
375 Hudson Street, New York, NY 10014

Philomel Books is a registered trademark of Penguin Random House LLC.
Library of Congress Cataloging-in-Publication Data
Names: London, C. Alexander, author. | Morrison, Frank, 1971– illustrator.
Title: The adventures of Wrong Man and Power Girl! / words by C. Alexander London ;
illustrated by Frank Morrison.
Description: New York, NY : Philomel Books, an imprint of Penguin Random House LLC,
[2018]
Summary: Although Wrong Man tries his best to help, he always seems
to make things worse but his faithful sidekick—and daughter—is there to save the day.
Identifiers: LCCN 2017020623 | ISBN 9780399548932 (hardcover)
| ISBN 9780399548949 (epub) | ISBN 9780399548956 (epib)
| ISBN 9780399548963 (kf8)
Subjects: | CYAC: Superheroes—Fiction. | Fathers and daughters—Fiction.
| Imagination—Fiction.
Classification: LCC PZ7.L8419 Adv 2018 | DDC [E]—dc23
LC record available at https://lccn.loc.gov/2017020623

Manufactured in China by RR Donnelley Asia Printing Solutions Ltd.
ISBN 9780399548932
10 9 8 7 6 5 4 3 2 1

Edited by Jill Santopolo.
Design by Ellice M. Lee.
Text set in Bookman Old Style and Blambot.
The art was done in acrylic on board.

WHEN DISASTER STRIKES, AND THE PEOPLE NEED A HERO, WHO DO THEY CALL?
OH NO! THERE'S A FIRE!

YES, POLICE? JANICE AGAIN. THE CROOKS ARE HEADED WEST ON MAIN STREET.

BEHOLD, I HAVE PUT UNDERPANTS ON THE DOG! ON ALL THE DOGS IN TOWN!
I REALLY DON'T THINK THAT'S APPROPRIATE.

WRONG MAN ALWAYS KNEW HE WAS MEANT FOR GREATNESS.

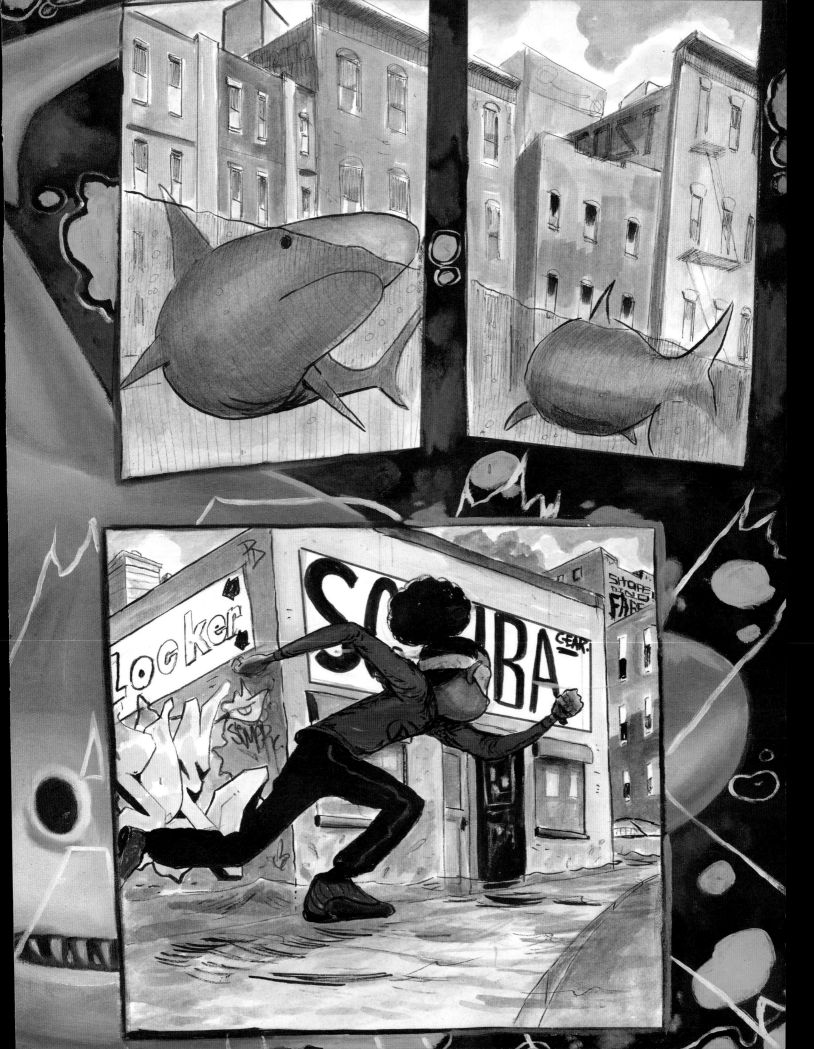

EVERYONE WAS GLAD HE HAD JANICE BY HIS SIDE.

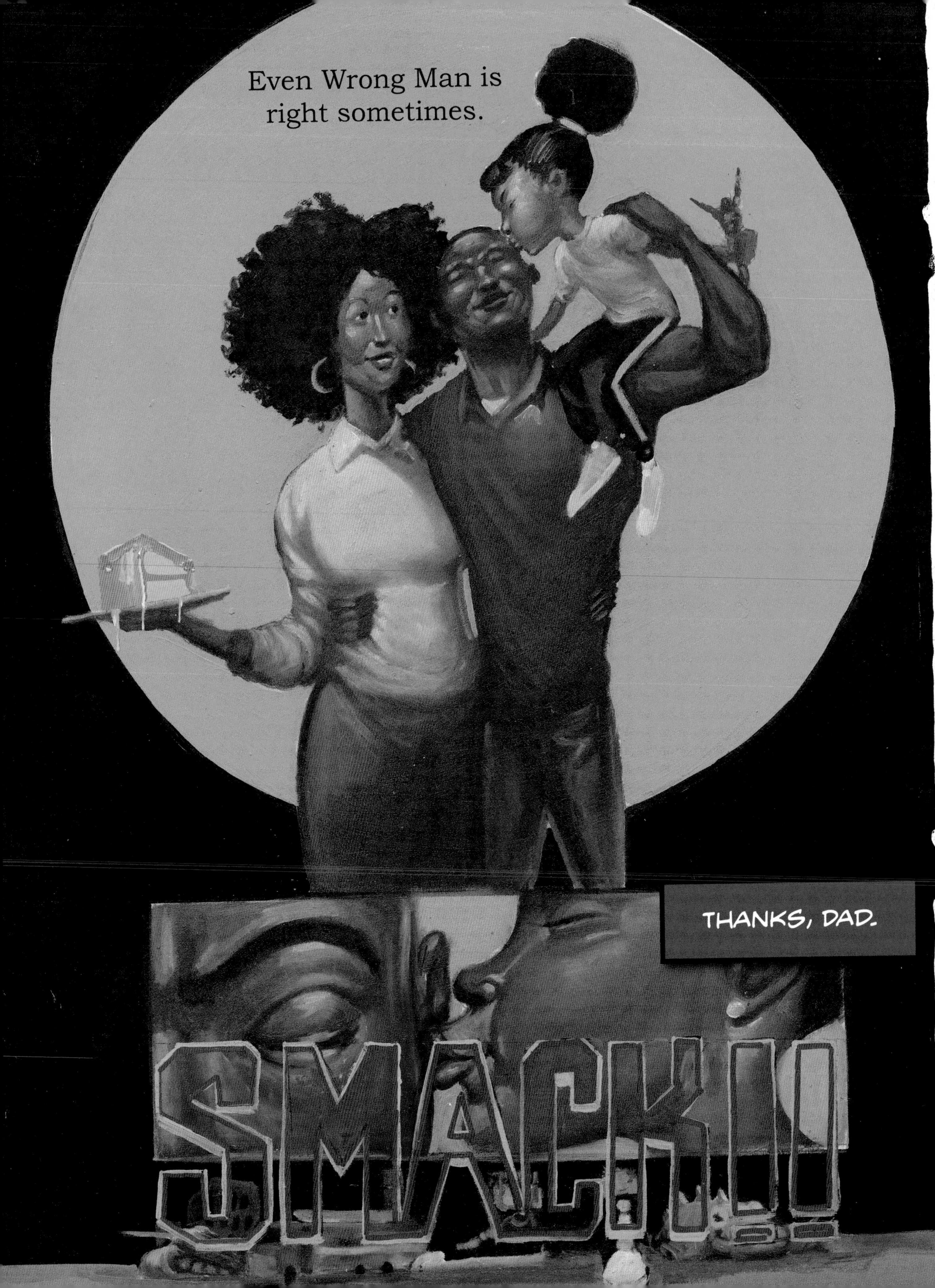
Even Wrong Man is
right sometimes.
THANKS, DAD.
SMACK!!